For my little fufus: Noah, Milo Zen and Lotus
and for my mom Katharyn and my sister Nefeterius

www.theenglishschoolhouse.com

ISBN: 978-0996001601

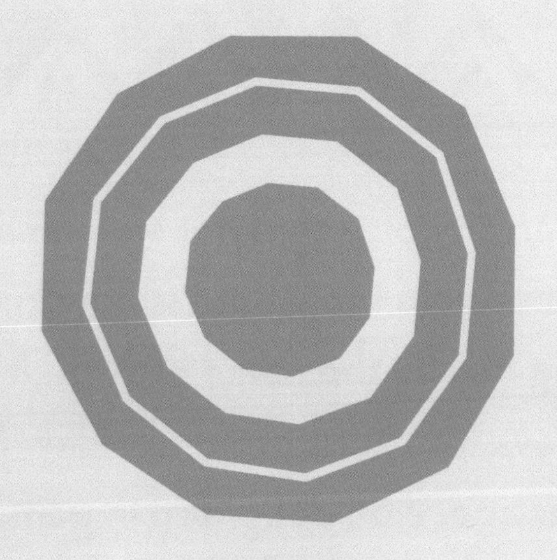

THE GHANAIAN *Goldilocks*

a story by **DR. TAMARA PIZZOLI**

In the West African city of Accra not so long ago, in a country that was once called Gold Coast but is now known as Ghana, there lived a young boy by the name of Kofi. It is a name given to many Ghanaian boys who are born on Friday. Much like other children around his age, Kofi delighted in games and fun.

He could most often be found down on the beach with his friends finding seashells just the right size for playing Pombo, perfecting his handstands in the water, or lying belly up in the sand wondering about the things his mama said would take time to understand.

When it was time to call her son in for lunch or dinner, Kofi's mother Abena rarely had a hard time spotting him. Having spent the better part of each day outside, the sun had soaked up the dark pigment in his hair, eventually leaving him with a healthy patch of nearly blonde coils.

As Kofi grew, so did his hair. It grew and grew until it twisted and stretched like the locks of some of the fishermen who caught and sold seafood by Elmina castle in Cape Coast.

Sista Adjowa, who crafted her own shea butter by hand and sold it at the Makola market by Kofi's house, had been the one to give him the nickname.

"I think we might have a blonde one on our hands, eh now Abena?" she laughed tugging and pulling one curl and letting it spring back suddenly. She tussled Kofi's tresses and attempted to run her fingers through it.

"I think a better fitting name for you, sweet Kofi, is Goldilocks, at least 'til you cut it all off." And it stuck.

Before long everyone in Kofi's part of town and many others outside of it knew the brown boy with the blonde hair as Goldilocks. Though it didn't bother him much to be called by a nickname, Goldilocks did notice that his hair made it difficult for him to get away with much of anything.

But they certainly didn't stop him from trying.

Like the time he and his friends accidentally kicked the ball into his neighbor Sista Francine's yard and Goldilocks jumped the dividing wall to get it instead of knocking on the door and asking permission first. His mama knew about it before he made it back to his family's side.

"Sista Francine called and asked if you'd kindly notify her before inviting yourself onto her property," his mama yelled from inside the kitchen just after he'd planted both feet on their pavement.

"Alright, mama!" he replied.

Or the time his mama sent him to do the shopping and Brah Yaw from the fruit stand told him he could help himself to three coconuts. A fourth somehow ended up in his sack.

When he returned his mama was waiting at the front door, and he hadn't even gotten all the way inside the gate before she started in. "Seems to me an arithmetic lesson may be in order. Brah Yaw said you mistook four for three?"

Stunned, the child mumbled and fumbled his words, searching for an explanation. "No use in trying," his mama began. "I'm your mama, this neighborhood is your family, a big family, and I'm always gonna know. Now go take that coconut back to Brah Yaw and say what needs to be said. Go on now."

"Yes mama, sorry mama," Kofi replied.

And so it happened that weeks and months passed and everything was as it should have been, until the day Mama Abena was making spinach stew and jollof rice, and she ran out of tomatoes.

“Kofi, please run next door and ask Sista Francine if we can borrow some tomatoes.”

The boy did as he was asked, but when he knocked on Sista Francine's door, there was no answer. There was also no point in going home and telling his mother the neighbors weren't home. He knew she'd just send him to the next neighbor's house, so there he went. The home had been all but abandoned for some time.

Kofi knocked lightly on the door. There was no response, but the child noticed that the door was slightly ajar. Pushing ever so softly, just enough to peek into the kitchen, he spied three inviting bowls of homemade fufu and palm nut stew waiting on the counter.

The aroma was so delicious and tempting, not to mention it would be ages before Mama Abena's stew would be ready.
He still didn't even have the tomatoes!

"Just a taste," he told himself, rushing quickly inside and pushing the door closed behind him.

First Goldilocks sampled the fufu in the biggest bowl, and he nearly burned off his index finger and thumb.

"Ayeeee!" he cried.

Determined to have a taste of the dough and broth, Kofi tried the fufu in the medium sized bowl next. It was cool to the touch.
In fact, it was way too cold for his taste. Moving on, he tried the fufu in the little bowl, and it was perfect.

It was better than perfect. It was downright delicious, so delicious that before he could stop himself, Goldilocks had swallowed every single clump of fufu whole and was slurping down the savory soup.

"Mamin," he burped, which means "I'm full"
in his native language of Twi.

Kofi had every intention of going home right then, but the bright colors from the living room caught his eye. He moved toward the space slowly and cautiously, checking the door every so often to make sure no one was coming.

He approached a semicircle of three stools. Having eaten such a heavy lunch, the thought of relaxing for a minute or two didn't seem like a bad idea.

First Goldilocks had a seat on the large stool, but it was as hard as a rock. Next Goldilocks tried the medium sized stool that bore the carving of the Sankofa bird, but with four pillows stacked on top, it was nearly impossible for him to balance on the seat.

Finally Goldilocks tried the littlest stool, and it was just right. It was better than right. It was perfect... and so multifunctional! With his imagination it could instantly transform into a bed, or a horse, or a boat, or a pirate ship, or a trampoline!

Goldilocks jumped and jumped to his heart's contentment and then

THWAT!

The stool split in half, and there lay Goldilocks, flat on his rear in the middle of the mess.

"Aye!" he cried as he scanned the damage.

Had he followed his first mind, Kofi would have left the home right then and there, but curiosity got the best of him again. He'd seen most of the house, but not the bedrooms. "I'll just take a quick look," he said to himself as he brushed off his backside and walked into an enormous bedroom shared by three.

Straight away, his eyes were drawn to the intricate carvings on the doors of three wardrobe closets. Running his hands over the designs of the largest one, he decided to take a look inside. The heavy wood creaked as Kofi struggled to open the door, and the child stood a moment and marveled at what was inside. It wasn't the Western-inspired clothes or shoes that held his gaze, but a beautiful assortment of Kente cloth that stretched from the floorboard to the very top of the closet. Goldilocks permitted himself to stroke every cloth he could reach.

Being aware that his mother would soon begin to wonder about his whereabouts, Kofi rushed along to the medium sized closet, the door of which flew open at the slightest tug. Inside was an array of hats and head wraps, sandals and slippers, dresses, gowns, tunics, and, of course, Kente cloth. It all reminded him of Mama Abena. Leaving that closet door slightly cracked, Kofi finally stood in front of the very last closet, the little one.

Goldilocks grabbed both doorknobs with his two hands and pulled. Once open Kofi could see both clothing and toys were inside. He spent a minute or two fiddling around with the closet's contents: a zither, a wooden boat with fishermen, a drum, a xylophone made with three calabashes, a tambourine, tiny village people, and a flute. Not wanting to make too much noise or leave too much evidence, he tried to place the instruments and playthings exactly where he'd first found them. Just when he was about to close the closet door and leave he noticed the clothes, all of which seemed so remarkably familiar. He was sure he had some of the very same shirts and pants, even shoes!

"Maybe we even wear the same size," Goldilocks mumbled softly, and while thumbing through a small assortment of Kente cloth, he made a spur of the moment decision to try on a couple of things.

KEEP
OUT

At that very moment, the Osei family walked in the front door carrying the last load of moving boxes from their old home in Kumasi. It took Papa Akuffo no time at all to realize that something just wasn't right in the Osei house, but before he had a chance to speak, Mama Nassima and their son Kwaku gasped.

Papa Akuffo walked over to the counter, peered into his bowl of fufu, then announced in a booming voice,

"Someone's been dippin' their fingers in my fufu!"

Mama Nassima examined her bowl. "Someone's been in my fufu, too!" she exclaimed.

Wide-eyed, Kwaku shrieked, "Someone's been dippin' their fingers in my fufu...and it's all gone!"

GHANA
Move 4 U
Move 4 U
GHANA
GHANA
GHANA
Move 4 U

The family moved suspiciously into the living room where they were left flabbergasted by the entire scene. Papa Akuffo sat on his giant stool, and knowingly nodded.

"Mmmm-hmmmm....someone's been sittin' on my stool."

Mama Nassima didn't even have to sit to know what had happened—the small bottom print on the top pillow told her everything she needed to know.

Pointing and shaking her head in disbelief she cried, "Someone's been sittin' on my stool!"

Kwaku, understandably so, was the most shocked and shaken of all. "Someone's been sittin' on my stool, and they broke it in two!"

Meanwhile, Goldilocks had heard the front door close. He'd listened to the family and their conversation as they moved through their home. He stood frozen in a stranger's clothes, panicking, not knowing what to do. He had options, he thought to himself, eyeing the window.

He could hop out, run home, and no one would know the difference. No one would know it was he who'd been in the Osei home.

He had a decision to make.

KEEP

Anger and confusion led the Osei family to their bedroom, where Papa Akuffo noted his closet door had been left slightly open.

“Let me guess,” Mama Nassima began, “somebody’s been looking through your closet.” “You know it,” Papa Akuffo replied.

Mama Nassima walked over to her wardrobe closet and straightened a pair of sandals Kofi had left out of place.

“No surprise here,” she sighed, “someone’s been looking through my closet.”

The parents turned to find their son staring at another figure they hadn’t noticed was present in the room. As Kofi braced himself for the worst, Kwaku spoke, “Looks like someone has been going through my closet, and liked what they saw!”

Kofi stood trembling in front of the family. He’d made a decision. He’d chosen to listen to the subtle voice in his mind that was always there, the one that urged him to do the right thing, even when the consequences are unknown.

Frightened and unsure of himself, he tried to explain.
“I...I don’t...well I just....what happened was I....well I....”

Just then, there was a knock on the front door.

“Hold that thought,” Papa Akuffo told Goldilocks, eyeing him intently, “I want to hear every word of what you have to say for yourself.”

When he opened the front door, he was greeted first by Goldilocks' mother, Mama Abena. Behind her stood all the neighbors and even some friends from across town.

"I understand my son is here?" Mama Abena began.

"Mmmmm-hmmmm" chimed in Sista Francine.

"I told it! The child went in and didn't never come back out,
so I called his mama."

Papa Akuffo nodded.

"Well," Mama Abena said, "we figured this was as good a time as any to welcome you and your family to our neighborhood. Akwaaba! Welcome! And of course I came to get my son."

Papa Akuffo stepped aside and the neighbors filed in carrying an array of wonderful delights. There was jollof rice, plantain, kenke, maasa, kebabs, fufu, fried fish, sweet doughnuts and oh so much more.

The roar of laughter and good conversation soon filled the house completely. Goldilocks tapped his mother gently on her back, his head hung low.

She lifted his chin and silently walked him over to the Osei family.

Goldilocks spoke slowly and deliberately, “I am sorry I came into your home without permission. I should not have eaten your fufu, and I apologize for breaking your stool, and...”

Papa Akuffo interrupted him mid-sentence.

“You precious and precocious child. Remember this day and the lesson that you have learned—it is a lesson I along with many wise Ashanti elders in this room learned when we were around your age...It is my job to make you feel at home when you come to my house. It is *your* job to remember you are not at home.”

A burst of laughter erupted and shouts of agreement echoed through the home and could be heard all the way down the road and to the city limits of Accra...

some say it was all heard as far as Kumasi.

Printed in Great Britain
by Amazon